A TEMPLAR BOOK

Produced by The Templar Company plc,
Pippbrook Mill, London Road, Dorking, Surrey RH4 1JE,
Great Britain.

First published in the USA in 1991 by GALLERY BOOKS, an
imprint of W. H. Smith Publishers, Inc., 112 Madison
Avenue, New York, New York 10016.
First published in Canada in 1991 by W. H. Smith Ltd, 113
Merton Street, Toronto, Canada M45 1A.
Gallery Books are available for bulk purchase for sales
promotion and premium use. For details write or
telephone the Manager of Special Sales. W. H. Smith
Publishers, Inc., 112 Madison Avenue,
New York, New York 10016 (212) 532-6600.

Designed by Philip Hargraves
Printed and bound in Hong Kong

ISBN 0-8317-0994-4

The
Brave Little Bunny

Written by Angela Holroyd

Illustrated by David Anstey

GALLERY BOOKS
An Imprint of W. H. Smith Publishers Inc.
112 Madison Avenue
New York City 10016

Blueberry Bunny was very unhappy. He lived with his family, in a cosy burrow, deep in the side of Cricklewood Hill. He should have been quite content, but he wasn't.

You see Blueberry Bunny was the smallest rabbit for miles, with the most enormous ears. Worse still one of them always drooped slightly – and because of this none of the other rabbits would play with him. Even his own brothers and sisters felt ashamed of his awkwardness. He felt very lonely, especially now that it was Easter.

All the other rabbits had been excited for days at the thought of the Easter Egg Hunt. The chocolate eggs that were to be hidden on Easter Sunday had been given to Mrs. Clutterbuck hen at Cricklewood Farm for safe keeping. But now there was uproar at the farm – not only had the special eggs been stolen, but also Mrs. Clutterbuck's four new chicks. Everyone agreed that it had to be the work of naughty Rufus Fox. They were all very upset.

"Can't you do something about it?" one of the young rabbits asked Ragwort.

Ragwort was the strongest, biggest rabbit in the neighborhood. He was also the most unpleasant.

"You have to be joking!" said Ragwort shaking his head. "No one with any sense would pay *him* a visit."

"But someone has to do something," said a small voice. All heads turned and stared at the speaker, sitting a short distance away. It was Blueberry. Ragwort burst out laughing.

"Just listen to that!" he jeered. "And from someone who's even frightened of his own shadow!" Blueberry winced. It was true – lots of things scared him.

"Blueberry Bunny, Blueberry Bunny! Whatever he does, he always looks funny." Ragwort chanted loudly, and thumped his paw heavily on the ground.

Blueberry stood up and slunk off in the direction of Cricklewood Forest – the noise of laughter ringing in his ears. Two big tears plopped onto his whiskers. Blindly he stumbled into the undergrowth, and flopped down in between the tangled roots of a huge tree.

"It's not fair!" he whimpered, wiping his wet fur.

"I quite agree!" A hooting voice, just above Blueberry's head made him jump. Blueberry looked up and there, on a branch, sat the most miserable owl he had ever seen.

"Shouldn't you be in bed at this time of day?" asked Blueberry, surprised to see a night owl awake.

"That's just it," moaned the owl. "The fact of the matter is – I can't sleep." He flew down on to the ground near Blueberry and held out a wing. "Allow me to introduce myself," he said. "I am Oscar Owl."

"And I am Blueberry Bunny," said Blueberry, shaking the owl's wing.

"How do you do Blueberry," said Oscar. "And what appears to be the problem?"

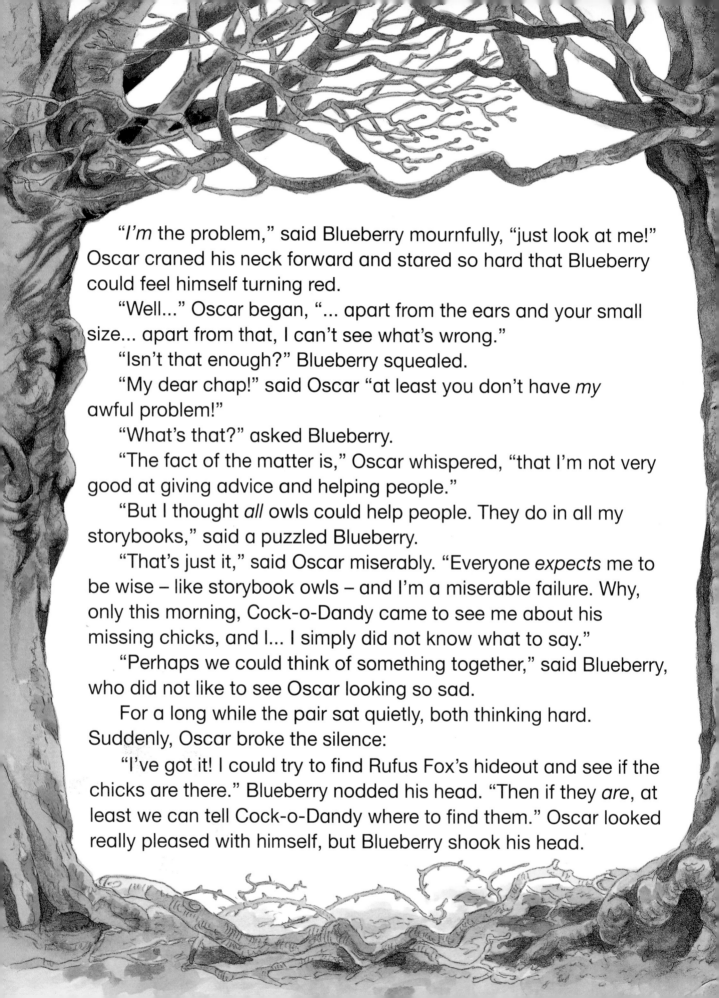

"*I'm* the problem," said Blueberry mournfully, "just look at me!" Oscar craned his neck forward and stared so hard that Blueberry could feel himself turning red.

"Well..." Oscar began, "... apart from the ears and your small size... apart from that, I can't see what's wrong."

"Isn't that enough?" Blueberry squealed.

"My dear chap!" said Oscar "at least you don't have *my* awful problem!"

"What's that?" asked Blueberry.

"The fact of the matter is," Oscar whispered, "that I'm not very good at giving advice and helping people."

"But I thought *all* owls could help people. They do in all my storybooks," said a puzzled Blueberry.

"That's just it," said Oscar miserably. "Everyone *expects* me to be wise – like storybook owls – and I'm a miserable failure. Why, only this morning, Cock-o-Dandy came to see me about his missing chicks, and I... I simply did not know what to say."

"Perhaps we could think of something together," said Blueberry, who did not like to see Oscar looking so sad.

For a long while the pair sat quietly, both thinking hard. Suddenly, Oscar broke the silence:

"I've got it! I could try to find Rufus Fox's hideout and see if the chicks are there." Blueberry nodded his head. "Then if they *are*, at least we can tell Cock-o-Dandy where to find them." Oscar looked really pleased with himself, but Blueberry shook his head.

"That's not any good. None of the farm birds, not even the great Cock-o-Dandy, would go far into Cricklewood Forest – let alone near that wicked fox. Why even Ragwort is scared of him!"

"I told you I wasn't wise!" said Oscar looking glum again.

"But you are. It's a very good idea of yours to find the hideout, if we *both* went, you could distract Rufus Fox, while I rescue the chicks." said Blueberry, forgetting his usual cowardliness.

"But *how* will you rescue them?"

"I don't know yet, but we'll think of something," said Blueberry.

Just then Blueberry noticed that the sun was going down.

"I'd better be going home now," he said, suddenly feeling scared. "I'll come back early tomorrow."

"Good idea!" said Oscar.

The next morning Blueberry's mother was surprised to see him up and dressed so early. Just as the sun was rising, he set off for Cricklewood Forest. Oscar was sitting on the same branch as the night before, waiting for him. He yawned widely.

"I've spent most of the night reading Sammy Squirrel's Riddle Book," he said sleepily. It struck Blueberry as a very strange way to spend the night, but he didn't want to say so.

"And that's not all," said Oscar, hardly able to contain his excitement. "I've found Rufus Fox's hideout, and what's more Mrs. Clutterbuck's chicks *are* there."

"Did you see them then?" asked Blueberry.

"No, but Rufus was outside very late last night, gathering herbs, and I heard him muttering to himself about how parsley and sage would go very nicely with baby chicken!"

Blueberry shuddered. "I think we'd better get going quickly," he said. "Before it's too late!"

Deeper and deeper the pair traveled through the woods. Blueberry didn't like the gloom, or the silence, very much. On and on they went until Blueberry could hardly see where he was going. He kept on tripping over tangled tree roots and crashing into scratchy bushes. It was only the thought of the poor baby chicks that made him determined to carry on.

Eventually the pair halted. To Blueberry's surprise, ahead he could see nothing but dark green pools – murky water surrounded by reeds and plants. Now, the one thing Blueberry was *really* scared of was water. So you can imagine how he felt when Oscar pointed out Rufus Fox's hideout, sitting on a tiny island surrounded by a big pool. Blueberry groaned.

14

"Shush!" whispered Oscar, pointing his wing toward the island. There, outside a rickety shack, was the fox lighting a fire beneath an enormous cooking pot.

"But I don't like water," whispered Blueberry.

"Pooh!" said Oscar rather unkindly. "There's nothing to be afraid of!"

"Not for you maybe, you can fly over it."

"Well, you can walk over it," said Oscar. "There are some stepping stones on the other side."

The pair skirted around the island until they were facing the back of Rufus' shack. And there, sure enough, were the stepping stones, just visible through the reeds.

"But even so..." began Blueberry, who didn't like the look of the slippery stones. "How can I get through the front door of the shack without Rufus seeing me?"

"I've thought of that," said Oscar proudly. "The fact of the matter is, that if you'd been just one teansy-weansy bit bigger then we would have been stuck, but being as small as you are, you can get through that tiny hole at the bottom." Oscar pointed to the back of the shack. The hole was so small Blueberry hadn't noticed it.

"But what if Rufus goes inside when I'm in there?" The thought made Blueberry quiver and quake.

"Don't worry about that. That is where the riddles come in," said Oscar mysteriously. "And when you have rescued the chicks, hide them in this hollow tree and hoot like an owl." He pointed his beak toward a large tree behind them.

Before Blueberry had time to protest any further, or to tell Oscar that he couldn't hoot, his friend had flapped his wings and disappeared.

Rufus Fox was bending over the cooking pot, when Oscar landed on a branch above his head.

"Good morning, Mr. Rufus!" hooted Oscar loudly, making Rufus jump. "And what a beautiful day it is."

"It's a more beautiful day than you think," said Rufus slyly, casting a wicked glance back at his shack, and wiping his hands on his dungarees.

"Yes siree! A very tasty day!" he grinned, showing a row of needle sharp teeth. "But I'm surprised to see you up Mr. Owl – don't your kind usually sleep when the sun's up?"

"The fact of the matter is Mr. Rufus, that I could not sleep. You see, I came across a number of riddles and, for the life of me, I can't work them out. So I thought to myself, 'Who do I know who is clever. Oh yes! I'll go and see Mr. Rufus – he's clever', I thought."

"Well now, you've sure come to the right place," said Rufus, flattered at being thought clever. "I like a good riddle and it will pass the time away until my water is ready." He sat down on a fallen log and grinned his evil grin.

"What shines but is never polished?" asked Oscar.

"That's easy! The sun, of course," Rufus answered quickly.

Better give him a hard one, thought Oscar.

"What is the biggest ant in the world?"

Rufus had to think hard, but finally he got it.

"A giant."

Oscar looked deliberately blank.

"A GI–ANT – get it?"

Meanwhile, Blueberry was wobbling on the second stepping stone. The next stone seemed a long way off. He dared not think about how deep, or how cold, the water was. Gritting his teeth he took a deep breath and...FLUMPETYJUMP, he landed safely. Just one more to go and he would be on the island. He wobbled a bit more then, holding his breath he leaped forward again. FLUMPETYJUMP, FLUMPETYJUMP! He had made it!

Keeping as low to the ground as possible, he crept toward the back of the shack. Very quietly he squashed himself through the tiny hole. For the first time in his life, he was glad he was so small and that his ears were bendy.

Inside, in the gloom, Blueberry could see a sack by a pile of potatoes – something inside it was wriggling! Quickly he undid the piece of string at the top and lifted out the startled chicks, one by one. They blinked and were about to cheep cheerily when Blueberry held up his paw. "Shush!" He pointed to the tiny hole. As fast as he could, he pushed each one through. Then he placed four potatoes in the sack, did up the string and looked around for the stolen eggs. He found them in a bag in the corner, which he had to push hard through the tiny hole. Finally, he squeezed himself through and joined the chicks.

"I'm going to carry you over to that tree," he whispered. "No one must utter even the smallest cheep, or we will all get eaten by the fox!" They all closed their beaks tightly, in fright!

Blueberry bravely carried each chick over, one by one, taking the eggs with him on the first crossing. Once they were in the tree, he opened his mouth and made a very strange sound – a little like a hoot but more like a croak! Nevertheless, Oscar heard it and heaved a great sigh of relief – he was running out of riddles.

"Well, I'll be off now Mr. Rufus," he said as casually as possible, "and thank you for helping me." He couldn't resist adding, "In fact, you have been more help than you realize!"

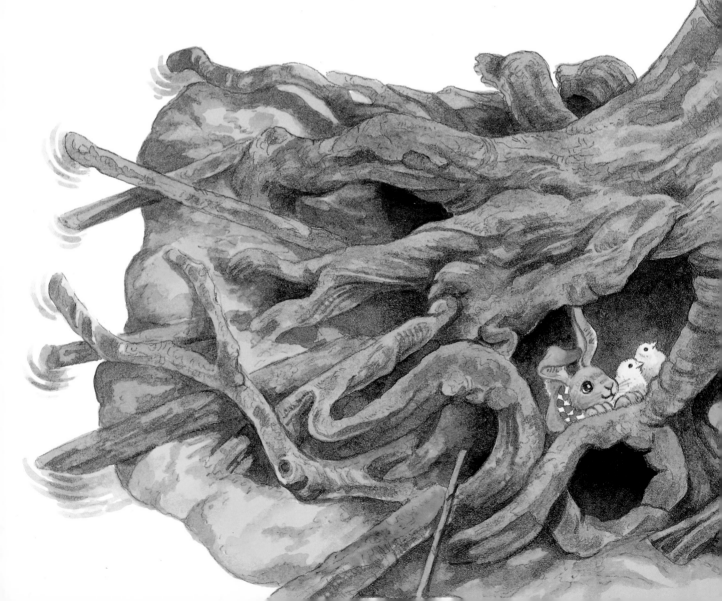

Rufus headed into his shack and dragged the sack outside. It seemed heavier, but perhaps it was just his memory playing tricks. Meanwhile Oscar had flown straight to the hollow tree.

"Quick! Two of you climb onto my back. I'll be back for you others as soon as I can." As he soared high above the tree tops he looked down and hooted:

"Stay hidden!"

Fortunately Rufus Fox didn't hear him, for just at that moment he discovered what was really in his sack and let out a huge, angry roar. Every animal in the forest heard it.

"SOMEONE'S STOLEN MY LUNCH! WAIT 'TIL I GET MY TEETH INTO THEM!" Then it dawned on him. "THAT OWL! THAT STUPID, BLITHERING OWL. HE KEPT ME BUSY WHILE...WHILE..." He was so angry that he could not spit the words out. Roaring loudly, he began leaping around the fire, stamping his feet with rage. He was so furious that he didn't look where he was going and the next minute he hopped RIGHT INTO THE FIRE!

"Yao..ow!" he screeched in pain as he hopped and limped on his sizzling feet over to the water to cool them down.

Blueberry and the chicks heard all the noise and huddled closer together inside the tree waiting for Oscar. Suddenly, they heard a whirr of wings and he was back. The last two chicks scrambled onto his back.

"Hold tight with your claws and beaks!" he warned them as he took off into the sky again.

Blueberry was now alone, but he set off through the trees quite happily. The woods were still dark, but he was no longer afraid. He knew that he wasn't the coward he had once thought he was. After all, hadn't he managed to overcome his fear of water and make the fierce fox look very foolish?

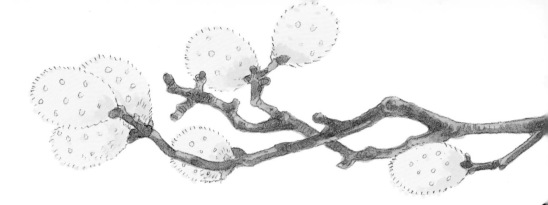

What a sound met Blueberry's ears as he came out of the trees onto Cricklewood Hill. Down below him, all the animals and birds had gathered to welcome him and were cheering at the tops of their voices.

"HOORAY FOR BLUEBERRY! BRAVO BLUEBERRY!"

Cock-o-Dandy had spread the word. Blueberry turned bright red as a crowd of rabbits rushed forward and lifted him onto their shoulders. Mrs. Clutterbuck came toward him beaming and clucking loudly.

"I can never thank you enough! I can never thank you enough!" she huffed and puffed over and over again.

"It was Oscar's plan," said Blueberry. "I couldn't have done it without his wise ideas."

"But my dear friend, the fact of the matter is, that if you hadn't been so small and so very, *very* brave, my plan would never have worked."

"Three cheers for the two heroes," Cock-o-Dandy crowed loudly, and everyone cheered again. Everyone, that is, except for Ragwort. He slunk away, annoyed that he was no longer the center of attention.

"They'll forget all about him tomorrow," he consoled himself. But they didn't. The next morning everyone wanted to play with Blueberry and asked him to be the leader of the Easter Egg Hunt. And he was never lonely – or cowardly – again.

The End